Lucy's Big Adventure

written and illustrated by

Isabella Velásquez

Dedication

For my mom, who believes in me and
supports me in everything I do.

Copyright © 2017 Lulu Author

ISBN 978-1-387-24501-7

Table of Contents

FORWARD

Lucy's Big Adventure is about the faith journey of Lucy, a Cocker Spaniel Puppy. Lucy has a lot of friends from all different breeds of dogs. Her two best friends are Bernadette, a Corgi and Therese, a Golden Retriever. Lucy and her friends are preparing for the Sacrament of Reconciliation at Sacred Heart Catholic Puppy School, where they attend 2nd grade.

Shortly after receiving the Sacrament of Reconciliation, Lucy and her friends decide to go on an adventure. The three pup friends had no idea how much they would learn along the way. They meet new friends and grow deeper in their faith. Although their journey is not easy, and they have to overcome many obstacles, they know that God is with them on this exciting and pawsome journey toward virtuous living.

Chapter 1

A "Pawsome" Sleepover

Ring, Ring! Went the school bell as the puppies rushed out the front doors of school! It was a long, busy Friday at Sacred Heart Catholic Puppy School. All the learning, test taking and studying, had made them tired. Some puppies went home for an after school snack and some went to the park to play for the rest of the afternoon. Today, Lucy and her friends went to the ice cream parlor with her grandma and also looked forward to a sleepover at Lucy's house.

It was almost summer and all the puppies were really excited! They were looking forward to swimming the doggy paddle in the town lake, hanging out with friends, and chasing the ball at the park. But, the puppy that is the most excited of all, is Lucy!

"Lucy, are you looking forward to summer?" said, Grandma. "Yes, of course I am!" barked, Lucy. "I have been waiting for Mom to have the baby for a long time! The baby is going to be born this summer, on June 16!"

Lucy's friends were all so happy for her.

"I am so excited it's a girl!" answered, Therese. "You've been praying for a baby sister for a long time!"

As Lucy, Therese, and Bernadette were walking into the ice cream parlor, they were talking about the new baby puppy. They hoped that the new pup would grow up to have close friends just like the three of them! Therese, Lucy and Bernadette have been best friends since pre-pup school.

"Look at the different flavors!" barked Bernadette referring to the ice cream. Her mouth watered as she decided what flavor she was going to choose.

"I can't decide! Oh...I guess I'll have birthday cake flavor," said Bernadette.

"I want chocolate!" exclaimed Lucy.

"I want mint flavor please," barked Therese.

"And I will pay for the ice cream," said Grandma. "It's my treat! Would you all like a waffle cone?"

"Yes, please!" The trio barked in unison.

Grandma could see that the girls had worked up quite the appetite at school. They were a hard-working bunch of pups!

As the girls were enjoying their ice cream treat, Lucy was thinking about her soon-to-be new baby sister.

She wondered, "How am I so blessed to be chosen to have a new baby sister? I wonder what she'll look like? I wonder what her favorite flavor of ice cream is?"

"Everything all right, Lucy, you look a little sad or confused?" barked, Grandma.

"Oh, yes, grandma...all pawsome." said Lucy.

As Lucy walked to the garbage can to throw away her trash, she couldn't help but look up at the beautiful sky. Suddenly she heard a tiny bark. It appeared to be coming from a small glimmer of light from up above. She thought, "Hmm, I wonder what that was? It's got to be all in my imagination."

After eating ice cream, the puppies were going to Lucy's house for a sleepover, but first, they walked grandma home and said good-bye.

"Goodbye Grandma," barked Lucy as she kissed her.

The puppies turned to walk away from Grandma's house.

"Ouch, this sidewalk is hot!" exclaimed, Bernadette.

"Let's swim at my house!" said, Lucy.

The pup friends set off to Lucy's house to ask her mother if they could go swimming before the sleepover.

At last, the girls arrived at Lucy's house and her mother opened the door and barked a joyful greeting.

"Hi, girls!" she said.

"Hi, Mrs. Spaniel," said Bernadette.

"Mom, it's hot, can we swim?" asked Lucy.

"It sure is hot! Yes, you can swim for an hour. Then you should come inside to prepare for your sleepover," said Mom.

"Let's go! First one in the pool is the luckiest pup!" barked, Lucy.

All the puppies ran to the pool and quickly jumped right in.

"Weeeeeeeeeee!!!!" exclaimed Lucy.

"It was really nice of your mom to let us swim," said Therese.

"She is the most amazing pup mom I know," said Lucy. All the girls gave a little giggle and agreed.

After an hour of splashing and playing in the pool, the puppies dried off and headed inside to prepare for the big sleepover.

When they got back inside the house, Lucy, Bernadette and Therese were super excited to show off their new pajamas their parents had bought them just for the sleepover!

"Let's do a puppy pajama fashion show!" exclaimed Therese.

"Great idea," agreed Lucy and Bernadette.

Each pup grabbed some accessories from Lucy's dress up box and did their best four-legged walk to show off their new pup pajamas!

"Lucy, I almost got those same pajamas!" Therese shouted when she saw Lucy's puppy ice cream pj's.

Bernadette was so proud to strut down the walkway showing off her new rainbow pup pajamas. The friends were amazed at the bright, beautiful colors!

Therese was the last pup to go. She grabbed a bright pink necklace and sunglasses to accessorize with her brand new heart and star pajamas. Bernadette and Lucy barked and said, "ooohh! I love the hearts and stars!"

After the girls finished their puppy pajama fashion show, they decided to read books while they waited for Lucy's mom to prepare dinner.

"Look at this book I found about all different types of puppy saints," said Bernadette

"You found a book about puppy saints, Bernadette?" questioned, Lucy.

"Yes, I sure did," barked Bernadette. "Look here, it discusses their life, and path to holiness."

"Oh wow! These names look familiar so familiar." said, Lucy.
"Yes, they do. There's St. Therese the Little Flower, St. Bernadette, and St. Lucy." barked, Bernadette.

"Our names are the names of saints!" Lucy said surprised.

The girls were really happy with their new discovery. They were honored to be named after great saints. Lucy suggested to her pup friends that some time they should thank their mom and dad for giving them their names.

The pizza was done cooling down in the kitchen, so the puppy friends made their way downstairs to get a bite to eat.

"This pizza is the best pizza in the world of pizzas!" shouted, Therese.

"How are you girls feeling about receiving the sacrament of Reconciliation this week?" asked Lucy's mother.

"Oh! That's right! We have our First Reconciliation on Wednesday!" remembered Bernadette chewing a piece of pizza.

All of the 2nd graders at Sacred Heart Catholic Puppy School have been preparing for weeks to receive the Sacrament of Reconciliation. They are all excited to receive the graces that come from confession.

The pup trio finished their pizza and yummy pupcakes for dessert. They quickly were tired and headed upstairs to set up their sleeping bags and get to sleep.

As the pups were laying awake they had many thoughts and discussions about their upcoming sacrament.

"What if I forget the Act of Contrition," Bernadette worried.

"It's okay, Bernadette. My daddy told me that if you forget the Act of Contrition, the priest will help you through it. He also said there is a booklet outside of the confessional with the Act of Contrition written inside of it. You can just bring that with you," said Lucy.

"That's what my mom does! My mom wasn't taught the Act of Contrition until she was much older in life and so she still forgets it sometimes," barked Therese.

"Thanks so much, girls, I feel better now," replied Bernadette.

The trio fell fast asleep.

The next morning, mom made pup donuts for breakfast. The puppies were very grateful to Lucy and her mom for the sleepover.

After she barked a good-bye to Therese and Bernadette, Lucy grabbed the last donut and ate it while she walked upstairs to her mom's room.

When she barked at the door, her mom opened it with a smile and said, "Yes, Lucy, how can I help you?"

"Mom, I need to talk to you about something. Can I come in?" asked Lucy.

"Yes, Lucy. How can I help you?" asked her mom.

"So, my friends and I were reading a book about saints last night and we discovered that all of our names are saint names. Did you and dad do that on purpose? Did you name me after a saint?" asked Lucy.

"Your father and I chose that name for you because we thought it was a very pretty name and we wanted to name you after Saint Lucy. Saint Lucy chose to love God at a very young age. She was also very courageous and defended her faith," explained Lucy's mother. "These are all of the things we hope for you."

"Oh wow! That's so interesting. Thank you so much for giving me this name and naming me after a great saint! I would like to learn more about St. Lucy. Can I read a little more about her in my room right now?" said Lucy as she shoved the last bite of her Boston Cream Donut into her mouth.

"Okay with me, but you have to come downstairs after you read about St. Lucy because we have to go to the store in 10 minutes." said Mom.

"Mom, I have one last question for you. Have you and dad decided on a name for the new baby yet?" asked, Lucy.
"No, not yet. We can't decide between Alison or Layla." said, Mom.

"Okay. I'm sure you and dad will decide on the best name for my baby sister. The two of you are great at picking out names! barked Lucy.

Lucy closed the door and went to read more about St. Lucy in her bedroom.

Chapter 2

The Big Discovery

Monday came quickly, and Lucy was ready for school, bright and early. She packed all her books and her homework in her backpack. She said goodbye to her mom and kissed her little brother. She then met her friends out front to walk to school.

"Hello, Therese and Bernadette." barked, Lucy.

"Good morning!" the friends replied.

"Hey! Guess what I found out when I got home from the sleepover?" said Bernadette. "I talked to my mom about my name and asked her if she and my dad named me after St. Bernadette and she said yes! Isn't that wonderful?" exclaimed Bernadette.
"Me too!" barked Therese. "I asked my mother and father if they named me after St. Therese the Little Flower and they said yes!"

"So we are all named after great saints! How wonderful!" said Lucy.

"How was your weekend, Lucy?" asked, Bernadette.

"Great, but also a little confusing. Mom and I discussed how I was named after Saint Lucy but I'm still wondering how she and dad knew that was supposed to be my name?" said, Lucy.

"I don't know, maybe God told them to name you Lucy." suggested, Therese.

"You might be on to something, Therese!" exclaimed Lucy.

"Whenever my parents have a big decision to make, my siblings and I see them praying. They teach us that all of their decisions are brought to God and he shows them what they are supposed to do. It only makes sense that they would ask God for guidance in naming me!" shouted Lucy.

"Thanks, Therese! I think you are right!" said Lucy.

"Come on pups, we are going to be late!" barked, Bernadette as they ran into school.

Therese and Bernadette ran ahead of Lucy. Before Lucy could run after them, she heard that same mysterious bark from up in the sky as she did on Friday at the ice cream parlor with grandma.

"My imagination is getting the best of me!" thought Lucy as she ran to class.

Back in class, the puppies were preparing for Reconciliation by having a retreat in their classroom.

Their teacher, Mrs. Dalmation, was focused on teaching them the proper steps for Reconciliation. She didn't want the pups to mess up or be too nervous.

She was also giving them time to examine their conscious. Mrs. Dalmation gave many examples of sins they might encounter and how they can avoid those sins in the future.

Mrs. Dalmation noticed the puppies were beginning to get tired from all of the preparation. It was time for a break.

"Alright class, it's time to take a 10 minute break. I'll blow the whistle at 9:30 so you'll know to come back inside the classroom. Enjoy your break!" Barked Mrs. Dalmation.

At recess, the puppy friends went to the library to read and talk more about the saints they were named after.

"Hey girls! Let's look up Saints Therese and Bernadette so you too can learn more about your namesakes." said Lucy excitedly.

The girls were searching through dusty old books and all of a sudden, Therese shouted, "I've got it! Hey Bernadette! I found the perfect book for you. It's all about Saint Bernadette!"

"Girls, girls be a little quieter please? The library is a quiet place." whispered, Mrs. Poodle, the librarian.

"Sorry, we will quiet down, Mrs. Poodle," said Bernadette.

"Oh wow! I've found a book all about St. Therese the Little Flower," whispered Therese.

The three pup friends discovered wonderful and exciting things about both St. Bernadette and St. Therese. They were especially surprised that at a young age both of these saints decided to live their life for God. Sadly, both of them also suffered and died at a young age from illness.

"Oh my!" exclaimed Therese in a whisper voice. "St. Therese and St. Bernadette both had visits and visions from our Blessed Mother, Mary!"

That morning while in the library, all three pup friends realized just how special their names truly are. They also knew they wanted to live up to the legacy of the great saints they were all named after.

Chapter 3

Sacrament Preparation

It was the end of the school day and Lucy was excited to go home and get ready for her first confession. At home, her family was working hard to prepare a special dinner for her.

"Mom, I'm excited and a little nervous to receive the Sacrament of Reconciliation tonight. Do you have any advice for me?" Lucy asked.

Mom replied, "When I'm feeling nervous, these are the things I do to prepare for Reconciliation:

- Take a deep breath
- Trust that God is with me
- Pray
- Think of all of my sins

"I have a prayer that might help you get over your nervousness, Lucy" said her mom.

Lucy was curious. "What is the prayer?" Lucy asked, wondering if it could really help her.

"The prayer I say is..."

"Jesus be with me, Jesus be with me, Jesus be with me." said Mom.

"When you call on God, he will come to help you. He will be with you and comfort you. All you need to do is ask." said Lucy's mom.

"Thanks a bunch of paws Mom!" barked Lucy.

"One more thing mom. Did you decide on a name for the new baby?"

"Yes, we've decided to name her, Layla." said Mom.

Lucy gave a big bark of joy and approval!

"Dinner!" Lucy's dad called from downstairs.

Dad had prepared Lucy's favorite meal. She was thrilled to see that he made her favorite sub sandwiches with extra pickles!

For dessert mom made Lucy's favorite Oreo Fudge Cookie Cake.

She was thankful and feeling so blessed by her family. They truly love her and want the best for her. What a pawsome way to celebrate her big night!

After dinner, Lucy ran upstairs to brush her teeth and get dressed!
"I am so nervous" barked Lucy as she passed her mom in the hallway.

"Lucy, remember the prayer I taught you." reminded her mom.

"I know, I know." replied Lucy. She was really nervous about telling Father Paw her sins, but she knew God was with her, always.

On the drive to church Lucy's family all prayed the rosary. When they arrived, they dropped Lucy off at the front and dad went to park the pupmobile.

When Lucy walked up, she found Therese outside the church sitting on a bench praying.

"Hi, Lucy!" barked Therese when she finished her prayers.

"Hi Therese! Do you know where Bernadette is?" asked Lucy.

"I just saw Bernadette a minute ago going into the church with Mrs. Dalmation," said Therese.

"So, do you think we're late!?" shouted Lucy.

"I don't think so, but we better head inside quickly!" Bernadette barked.

Chapter 4

Confession and an Opportunity

The pup friends ran right through the open doors of the church, and right into Mrs. Dalmatian.

"Lucy, and Therese!" cried Mrs. Dalmatian. I was looking everywhere for you two!"

Lucy was very sorry and she looked at Therese, she felt sorry too!

"Well," began Mrs. Dalmatian, "Let's get you girls lined up with the rest of the class."

While standing in line, butterflies started to form in Lucy's tummy making her nervous again. She looked out into the church sanctuary and saw her parents. They both gave her a big smile and a paws up. Lucy also thought about her little baby sister, Layla, to calm her down. She then repeated the prayer that her mother taught her and that really helped too.

It was Lucy's turn. Mrs. Dalmatian gave her a little nudge toward the open door to the right of the small puppy sized room. She slowly walked straight in.

It was comfortable, but not too comfortable. There was a chair for sitting on and also a kneeler for kneeling.

Lucy couldn't see Fr. Paw's face behind the confessional stall but suddenly she heard his soft voice say, "You can choose to sit, or kneel my dear." Lucy chose to kneel.

Lucy took a deep breath and began...

"Bless me father for I have sinned, it is my first confession, these are my sins......."

After Lucy finished with reconciliation, she found her parents waiting for her in the pew.

Lucy suddenly felt an overwhelming sense of relief as God's graces flowed through her. Lucy couldn't wait to talk to Therese and Bernadette because of something that Father Paw revealed to her during confession.

You see...Lucy had questions for Father Paw about her direction in life. He said that she and her friends would have to journey to the top of Paw Peak to find the answers to their questions. Fr. Paw said this journey will not be easy, but trust in God and do not be afraid.

Outside of the church, Lucy, Bernadette and Therese all ran up to one another and gave a joyful, happy bark! The pup trio were so happy after receiving the Sacrament of Reconciliation!

Lucy, Therese and Bernadette went to the ice cream shop to celebrate with their families.

At the ice cream shop, Lucy's mom gave her the most beautiful necklace. It was a large, round locket that had a window in it so you could see little charms inside of it.

"Each charm symbolizes you," explained Lucy's mom.

"The book charm symbolizes your love of reading, the cross symbolizes your faith, the aquamarine birthstone is for your birth month and lastly there is a beautiful, pawprint charm too!" Lucy's mom said excitedly.

Lucy loved it and gave her parents a great big puppy kiss! She was surprised to see that Therese and Bernadette received a similar locket necklace also!

Therese's locket charms were a heart, a cross and a pawprint. Bernadette's locket charms were a bow, a cross and a pawprint! They all loved and admired their necklaces.

Back at home, Lucy asked her mom if she could call her pup friends before bedtime. It was really important that she talk to them. She needed to tell them about her conversation with Father Paw.

"Sure thing, Lucy," said her mother. "Just a quick 10 minute phone call and then it's time for bed. We've had a long, exciting day and we all need our pup sleep."

Lucy quickly called her friends and shared with both Therese and Bernadette what Father Paw had revealed to her during her confession.

She explained how she was struggling with sins of impatience and frustration with her little brother and also with her mother and father. She noticed that she was saying things she didn't mean and even disobeying her mom and dad at times. She told Father Paw that she wonders if it's because she just isn't sure what she's supposed to be doing in her life and so she's taking her frustrations out on her family.

Lucy further explained to Therese and Bernadette, "Then Father Paw said that I'm much too young to have to worry about the rest of my life right now but that it is important to seek God's will in my life on a daily basis. He says this way, when the really tough decisions of life need to be made, I can more easily ask God for guidance."

Both Therese and Bernadette were amazed at what Lucy was telling them.

"The last thing that Father Paw told me was that I could venture up to Paw Peak and find some of my answers there. He said that the journey to Paw Peak has been known to reveal so many things to God's people." explained Lucy.

"I want to go with you!" Barked Therese.

"Me too," said Bernadette.

"Let's go on Saturday morning. First, we need to let our parents know we are going to take a little hiking adventure up Paw Peak so they don't worry about us." planned Lucy.

"Sounds like a great plan!" barked Therese.

After her phone calls, Lucy snuggled up in bed and fell fast asleep. She dreamed of what adventures she would encounter on their journey to Paw Peak.

Chapter 5

Preparation for the Journey

The rest of the school week seemed to go by so slowly. The pup trio just couldn't wait to go on their journey. Saturday morning finally arrived and Lucy woke up bright and early.

She packed her toothbrush, blanket, stuffed puppy, crackers and water in her pink backpack. Lucy was super excited to start out on her adventure up Paw Peak. She headed downstairs to say goodbye to her mom and dad.

"I made you some pup pancakes and a yogurt parfait so you can start out with a full belly." explained Lucy's mother.

"Thanks so much, mom! You're the best!" barked Lucy.
After breakfast, Lucy kissed her mom and dad goodbye and set out to get Therese and Bernadette.

Lucy gathered both of her friends and they began their fun and pawsome journey."

"Girls, do you remember what our goal is for this adventure?" asked Lucy.

"Yes! We sure do! Father Paw said that we can find the answer to our vocation in life and any other questions that we may have by traveling up to Paw Peak." explained Bernadette.

"That's right," said Lucy. "He also said that the journey will be hard but God will be with us."

The pup friends took a minute to make sure they had packed the essential items they might need on their journey.
Therese packed her blankie, toothbrush, chocolate candy, and a doggy bowl.
Bernadette packed flashlights, a compass, rain ponchos and doggy treats.

"Good thing you packed survival items for us, Bernadette!" Barked Lucy.

The pups then stood hand in hand and prayed a decade of the rosary before they set out to Paw Peak.

"Now let's go girls!" Shouted Therese.

Chapter 6

Marco the Bird

The puppies were about an hour into their journey when they came upon their first challenge... the dark woods. They've heard that there are a lot of animals in the dark woods.

"I don't think we should go this way, let's just give up and go home." said Bernadette, walking away.

"Bernadette." moaned Therese, "We can't give up now." she said as she ran after Bernadette.

When Therese gathered Bernadette and they returned to where Lucy stood, they saw her face. She wasn't worried or afraid.

Lucy said, "We have to go into the forest. It's the only way and we aren't giving up now. We can do this." barked Lucy, walking into forest. Therese and Bernadette followed behind her.

"Can, can, cccan we pray the Saint Michael prayer?" stammered Bernadette.

"Yes! That's a great idea!" said Therese.

The three friends stopped and held hands while they prayed,

"Saint Michael, the Archangel, defend us in battle, be our protection against the wickedness and snares of the devil. May God rebuke him we humbly pray and do thou of Prince of the heavenly hosts, by the divine power of God, cast into hell satan, and all the even spirits, who prowl about the world seeking the ruin of souls, Amen."

"I feel so much better now!" barked Bernadette.

The puppies were about a mile into the forest when they suddenly heard a cry and a chirp for help.

"Wait, listen." said Lucy as they stopped in their tracks.
"Www, wha what was that?" asked Bernadette as she hid behind Therese.

"It's okay, Bernadette." said Therese. "I think somebody needs our help! Let's go!"

The puppies raced to where the sound was coming from.

"Someone please help me out of this net!" cried a small animal.

Lucy jumped back and said, "Who was that?"

"Up here!" chirped a little bird caught up in a tree in a net.

"What happened little bird?" asked
Bernadette.

"I got trapped in this net, please help!" cried
the little bird.
"It's going to be okay, I'll help you!" said
Bernadette as she jumped up and gnawed at
the net tugging and pulling.

"Grruff! Chomp! Ruff!" Bernadette chewed
on the net until suddenly the bird fell out of
the hole in the net.
"Aaaaaaaaaaaaa!!!" cried the little bird.

"I'll save you!" Bernadette shouted as she
jumped up and gently grabbed the tiny bird
with her mouth. Bernadette opened up her
mouth and the bird swiftly jumped out and
landed safely on the ground.

"Yeah! Bernadette did it! She did it!" barked
Therese, hugging Lucy.

"Well, I have to thank you for saving my
life, pup." said the bird to Bernadette.

"It was my pleasure, little bird," replied Bernadette.

"By the way, what is your name?" asked Therese to the bird.

"My name is Marco," chirped the little bird. "Marco at your service!" chirped Marco.

"I'm Bernadette. This is Therese and Lucy." barked Bernadette.

All of a sudden, before she could say anything more, something amazing happened. Bernadette's necklace began to glow and she was being lifted up into the air.

"What in the world of puppies is happening?" said Bernadette, surprised.

Suddenly, the clouds parted and heaven opened up. There were angel puppies everywhere!

"Bernadette, you have saved little Marco from being trapped in that net." said a loud voice from heaven, "I'm very proud of you."

"Wow! Bernadette, you are glowing so brightly!" said Lucy, amazed.

Bernadette's puppy hair turned long with rainbow colors and she had golden wings. She was admiring her golden wings, when all of a sudden she was slowly lowered down to the ground with her eyes closed.

"Bernadette! Bernadette, wake up Bernadette!" Lucy shook Bernadette.

Bernadette slowly opened her eyes and sat up. "Wow! That was amazing! shouted Bernadette.

"You did it Bernadette! You saved the bird!" barked Lucy and Therese.

"Goodbye, Bernadette, Therese and Lucy!" chirped Marco. "I must be on my way. Thank you for saving me!"

"Bye, Marco!" barked Bernadette.

"Hope we see you soon!" cried Lucy to Marco.

"Look out for those nets!" shouted Therese.

The puppies had a long and exciting morning. While they thought about the fun they had they also wondered how and why Bernadette was transformed into a glowing rainbow puppy.

Was it because of the necklace? Was it because of the good deed she did when saving Marco the bird? There were so many questions unanswered. The puppies were looking forward to the next part of their journey.

Chapter 7

Farmdog Bernie

A couple hours had passed and the puppies came upon a farm.

"Ooh! Let's see if we can find a resting spot inside that big red barn," suggested Lucy.

The puppies were getting tired and needed to take a nap. They circled around to the front of the barn door and helped themselves inside.

They were amazed when they went inside and found a bunch of farm animals awake and enjoying lunch!

"Mooo! Baaaa! Quack! Neigh!" went the animals.

"Why is it so loud in here?!" shouted Bernadette, covering her ears.

"Because it's lunchtime!" barked Lucy.

Suddenly a little Shih Tzu pup came inside the barn and shouted, "What is all that racket!?

"Oh no! This must be his farm," shouted Lucy, referring to the little Shih Tzu puppy.

"You puppies, there!" said the farmer pup. "What are you doing in my barn?"

"Excuse me, um, farmdog, said Lucy, "we were wondering…"

The farm pup quickly corrected Lucy and said, "My name is Bernie!"

"Oh, Bernie, we are so sorry we got into your farm." replied Lucy.

"Yes, we are so sorry," said Therese.

"Mr. Bernie," begged Bernadette. "We have been on a long journey today and we are getting so tired. Would you mind if we took a little rest here in your barn? We just need a quick little nap so we can continue our mission."

"Where are you headed to?" asked Bernie, impatiently.

"To Paw Peak. Do you know where that is?" asked Lucy.

The puppy farmer paused to think about it. Then he said, "Oh yea, Paw Peak is that steep mountain with a beautiful waterfall. It's also rumored that there are serpents guarding the path to the waterfalls. Very few pups have ever made it up to Paw Peak."

The puppies gasped at the idea of serpents.

"Why do you need to go to Paw Peak anyway?" asked Bernie.

Lucy, Therese, and Bernadette shared all the details about Father Paw's message to Lucy and why they've decided to take this journey up to Paw Peak.

"WOW! That is quite the story," said Bernie.

"So, can we stay here for the afternoon?" asked Therese with pleading eyes.

"Sure thing, Pups!" said Bernie.

That afternoon when the pups woke up from their nap, they could smell the most delicious smells coming from the farmhouse kitchen.

"Puppies! Come and get your freshly made pancakes!" called Bernie.

"Pancakes are my favorite!" Bernadette yelled as the puppies ran to the farmhouse.

When their afternoon snack was finished, the puppies packed their stuff up and said goodbye to their new pup friend, farmer Bernie.

"Bye, pups! Come and visit again soon!" barked the little farmdog.

"Thanks for all your help! Oh, and where is Paw Peak?" shouted Lucy.

"Go straight until you see a big oak tree!" said Bernie. The puppies set off toward the big oak tree.

Chapter 8

Christopher the Squirrel

As the puppies continued on toward the Big Oak Tree, Bernadette suddenly felt little drops of water on her head.

"What was that?" asked Bernadette. The little drops of water kept on falling from the gray sky.

"Oh no! It's rain! Run!" shouted Therese.

Thunder and lightning came fast and was loud and scary. The puppies ran, until Lucy spotted the big oak tree with lights in it.

"The oak tree! I found it! Let's GO!" ran Lucy.

Lucy, Bernadette and Therese stopped at the foot of the oak tree and looked up. They noticed a little tree house built neatly within the branches.

The rain was still coming down, hard. The puppies one at a time, climbed the big tree, until they came to the front door of the tree house.

"Let's knock on the door." said Lucy as she barked at the door.

Suddenly the little door opened and inside stood a squirrel.

"Oh, hello! Bernie, the farmdog told me you were coming!" said the little squirrel, "Quick, come inside! It is raining really hard!"

The puppies were so relieved and a little confused.

"You expect us to go in your little house?" asked Lucy, confused.

"It's really okay. You can find somewhere else to take shelter then if you don't want to come inside," said the squirrel, closing the door.

"NO! Wait!" barked Therese, "We will stay until the storm passes."

"Are you sure we can fit, Therese?" doubted Lucy.

"I know we can." said Therese already trying to squeeze into the door. "I think I need help though."

The puppies and the squirrel helped pushed Therese into the little house. Soon, Lucy, Bernadette and Therese were inside the house having cups of hot chocolate.

Therese asked, "So, what is your name little squirrel?"

"My name is Christopher," he said.

"My name is Therese, that is Lucy, and this is Bernadette. We are on a mission to discover our direction in life and our vocations. We hope to find our answers at Paw Peak," barked Therese happily.

Christopher paused to think about Paw Peak before speaking. He then shared with the puppies all that he had heard about Paw Peak. There were plenty of wonderful things but also some rumors he had heard about others never making it all the way to the top.

For many reasons, those who tried to get to the top of Paw Peak had to turn around and go home. He was trying to encourage the pups but also let them know that this journey was going to be tough.

It wasn't before long that the pups realized the rain had stopped. They went outside to investigate a little closer.

"Oh Wow!" shouted Bernadette, "Look at that beautiful rainbow over there!"

Just as the puppies and Christopher turned their heads to see the rainbow, something wonderful happened.

Therese was suddenly being lifted up into the air.

There was a bright light and once again heaven opened up, there were hundreds of angel puppies and a loud voice said, "Therese, you trusted my friend, Christopher the squirrel, to let you in his house so you and your friends would be safe from the storm. You have shown great faith."

Then, Therese had golden wings and her fur turned into rainbow colors just like Bernadette's did earlier today when she rescued little Marco bird.

"WOW! This is super cool and magical!" Therese exclaimed.

Therese then returned to her normal puppy self again and was slowly lowered back down to the ground.

"Therese! Therese!" said Bernadette "You did it, Therese! You demonstrated great virtue just like I did when I earned my golden wings and rainbow hair!"

Lucy also joined in with excitement and said, "You trusted that God would keep us safe and dry from the storm and He sent us a friend to help us. God sent us Christopher, the squirrel!"

It was an exciting day for the puppies and the squirrel. They played some games like "Simon and Jude Says" and also the Game of Life, Puppy Edition!

"What a wonderful, fun-filled day!" said Therese.

"I'm exhausted," said Bernadette. "Would you mind if we stayed in your tree house for the night, Christopher?"

"Sure thing, puppies. I'd be happy to help you all out with a warm place to sleep for the night." said Christopher.

Christopher brushed his teeth, Bernadette put on her PJs, Therese brushed her fur and Lucy decided to sleep outside under the stars.

The next morning, Bernadette jumped out of bed. She was hoping she would smell freshly baked, warm pancakes, but instead, she smelled…. acorns?

"Pups! Come down and get breakfast!" shouted Christopher.

Therese came down the wooden stairs looking so sleepy.

"Did we have to wake up so early?" moaned Therese.

Christopher had set the table for the pups. Each place setting had a leaf placemat, a plate and a cup. In the middle of the table was a bowl of acorns!

"Where is the fruit, pancakes and syrup?" asked Bernadette looking confused.

"Acorns are for breakfast." said Christopher looking very pleased to host a meal.

"Sorry, but puppies don't eat acorns." said Lucy with a sad look on her face.

"We brought some fruit with us." Therese opened up her pup-pack to reveal a bunch of fruit the puppies saved.

"I have not tried fruit before." said Christopher.

"Would you like to try some fresh fruit?" said Bernadette.

"I would LOVE to!" replied Christopher. "Will you try acorns?" he asked with pleading eyes. There was a pause of silence and everything stood still.

"I will try it." barked Therese going for an acorn and ate it.

She chewed silently and said, "I.........LOVE IT! Barked Therese.

Soon, the puppies and squirrel had full tummies to start their day. It was time for the puppy trio to say goodbye and begin the second day of their journey.

"Bye pups! I hope you can find the answers you're looking for at Paw Peak!" shouted Christopher.

"Thanks for letting us stay in your tree house!" barked Lucy.

The puppies once again set on their journey to Paw Peak.

Chapter 9

The Deep, Dangerous Gorge

"Christopher the squirrel told us to look out for a bridge," said Lucy as she lead the group through the forest and up the mountain.

As they walked, the puppies were recalling all that they've experienced on their journey so far.

They had rescued a baby bird, met an awesome farmdog named Bernie and his farm animals, and they made a new squirrel friend who was a gracious host!

The pups soon realized that all of their food was eaten up, and they were quickly starting to feel hunger pangs just a few hours after leaving Christopher's tree house.

"I'm very hungry and tired," complained Therese and Bernadette.

"Look! I see a little river over there and it looks like some fresh berries next to the riverbed!" cried Lucy.

The puppies took turns drinking from the river and enjoyed mouthfuls of berries.

"You have a berry smile, Therese," laughed Bernadette.

"You do too!" said Lucy to Bernadette.

The three puppy friends laughed as they filled their tummies with a little snack.

"We should get going now. I'm sure we are almost there!" barked Lucy. The puppies walked another hour up the mountain when suddenly they came to the bridge.

As the puppies approached the bridge, they all gasped. The bridge somehow had broken and snapped. Beneath it was a deep, dangerous gorge.

"The bridge is broken. What are we going to do now?" asked Bernadette.

"I don't know." said Therese feeling hopeless.

"Maybe there is another way around," barked Lucy. "We can't give up now!"

Suddenly, Lucy heard a familiar voice from up above.

"Need help down there?" asked an angel puppy. The angel puppy flew down to meet the puppies.

"You are an angel puppy!" said Lucy. "Are you the puppy that's been following us on this journey?

"Indeed I am. My name is Rose," said the angel puppy.

"Rose, we need help to get across to the other side," said Bernadette.

"Oh, puppies." said Rose, "You already have the power inside of you."

"What do you mean?" asked Therese.

Rose said, "I have been watching you the whole time from heaven. Remember when Bernadette saved that little baby bird? And then how Therese demonstrated the virtue of faith when she trusted Christopher, the little squirrel?"

"Yes," barked the puppies in unison.

"This 'power within us' that you speak of. Does it have anything to do with the rainbow colors and golden wings that appear each time one of us makes us a virtuous choice?" asked Therese.

"I also noticed that our necklaces glow too!" shouted Bernadette.

"Exactly!" said Rose, "When you make an act of virtue and trust in God, you earn your golden wings and your ability to fly."

"That's incredible!" barked Therese.

"But there's just one thing," said Bernadette. "Lucy hasn't earned her wings yet."

Lucy put her head down. She felt sad that she hadn't earned her golden wings yet.

"Wait! I've got it! I think we can fly over the broken bridge on our own!" exclaimed Therese.

"Yes! I can hold Lucy while we fly over the deep gorge!"

"That's a great idea," said Rose

"But how do we make our wings appear? We don't know how to control our golden wings." exclaimed Therese.

"Oh, I almost forgot to tell you! Once you've earned your rainbow wings, the way you get your rainbow wings to appear again is by chanting 'Catholic Puppies' at the same time," instructed Rose.

The puppies all stood together while holding hands and said, "CATHOLIC PUPPIES!"

Then suddenly, Bernadette and Therese's glowing wings appeared. Bernadette swiftly picked up Lucy and carried her to the other side of the canyon with Therese following close behind them.

When the puppies landed, they could see miles of mountains and rolling hills.

"Thank you so much for helping us get across that canyon, Rose!" barked Therese happily.

"You're welcome Catholic Puppies!" said Rose as she was lifted up and vanished out of sight.

Chapter 10

The Serpents

The puppies knew that they would eventually come upon the serpents that farmdog Bernie had told them about. The thought of it made them shudder with fear.

After a few hours of hiking through the mountains, they came upon a cave. Just beyond the cave they could see Paw Peak.

"We're almost there!" shouted Therese.

"Can we just please stop and go home now?" whispered Bernadette covering her paws over her eyes as they approached the cave.

"We have to find out what we're meant to do in life." Lucy said, barking so loudly that it shook the cave.

The puppies jumped back when they heard slithering noises from inside the cave.

Suddenly, they could see two long shadows lurking at the back of the cave.

Lucy couldn't believe her puppy eyes at the sight of two serpents staring right at her.

"Run Lucy, run!" screamed Therese.

Bernadette and Therese hid in the bushes and took cover.

"Hhhissss!" said the serpents. "You barked too loudly and disturbed our nap!"

Lucy was frozen with fear and didn't know what to do.

"Now we're going to have to eat you!" hissed the serpents.

"Well, are you sure I look tasty?" asked Lucy to distract the serpents.

"I never ate a puppy in my life before." said one serpent to the other, licking his lips.

"Well, today is not your day because you are not going to eat me!" said Lucy.

Therese and Bernadette gasped as they watched from the bushes.

The serpents hissed again and tried to lunge forward at Lucy. Lucy dodged and jumped and then ran in circles. She continued to run in circles and confuse the serpents. She went around and around until the serpents were so dizzy they bumped into each other and fell over.

"Ha! My God is always by my side to help me and protect me when I'm in trouble. You two serpents underestimated me and my God!" exclaimed Lucy.

This act of bravery made Lucy's locket start to shine brightly.

Suddenly her golden wings appeared and she was lifted up high in the sky.

Bernadette and Therese jumped out of the bushes and began cheering! Lucy had earned her golden wings!

Suddenly the clouds parted and heaven appeared more brightly than ever. The pups were amazed to hear a loud voice from heaven speaking to Lucy saying, "Lucy, you were so brave when you chose to defeat the serpents. This is very pleasing to me."

Hearing this made Lucy smile the biggest smile on her pawsome face.

Lucy then looked to Bernadette and Therese and waved her paw and pointed to her locket urging them to join her in rainbow form.

Both Bernadette and Therese, held onto their lockets and said together, "CATHOLIC PUPPIES!"

A golden light shown as, Bernadette and Therese were lifted up and golden wings appeared as they joined Lucy.

Suddenly Lucy's face had a flower appear on her cheek, while Bernadette's face had a star and Therese had a heart. The pups had earned their virtue marks!

Before they knew it, a rainbow shot across the sky and landed right where the serpents were lying down in the cave and it encircled them.

The serpents woke up and shouted, "What is happening!?"

The rainbow suddenly vanished into a flash of light and sparks filled the cave as the serpents disappeared.

The puppies were then gently lowered back to the ground in their normal puppy form.

"We did it!" barked the puppies as they all clapped paws.

It had been a long morning for the Catholic Puppies. They decided to take a break for lunch before heading to the top of Paw Peak.

Chapter 11

Paw Peak

After the girls finished their light lunch of berries and drank from the stream, they packed up their stuff and they headed out.

The puppies could tell that they were close because the climb up the mountain became very steep. The air was thinning and the puppies began panting.

"Can.... We.... Take.... A break now?" huffed Bernadette.

"We are almost there I can feel it!" barked Lucy.

The puppies climbed, and climbed until they could finally see the most amazing waterfall with sparkling water rushing down the falls. "It is so pretty!" gasped Therese jumping up off the ground.

"Now, let's find out what we are all here for." said Lucy.

The puppies spread out and began looking in lots of different places like under a rock, in the grass, they also looked in the water!

Lucy sat gazing into the water saying, "How will I ever know what my vocation in life is, and all these other questions I have inside of me?"

Lucy then pulled out a picture she brought with her on the journey. It was a picture of her family. She cried a little tear because she missed them so much and was looking forward to going home to tell them all about her journey.

Something amazing happened when her tears dropped into the water from the falls. The clouds parted and the heavens opened up and little angel puppies appeared with Rose beside them.

"Wow!" barked Lucy.

"Lucy!" said a loud voice from heaven.

The puppies came running over to see what was going on. A big figure of a puppy stood in the middle of all the angel puppies. They knew right away that it was Puppy Jesus!

"You have come all this way to ask me some questions?" said Puppy Jesus.

"We were wondering how we are supposed to know our vocation in life? What are we supposed to do when we grow up and how do we know what God wants?" said Lucy as she was out of breath.

"These are all very good questions, Lucy," barked Puppy Jesus. "God has given you the Holy Spirit to be your guide. When you pray, ask the Holy Spirit to help you in your daily life. The Holy Spirit can support you with the small decisions and big ones too!"

Puppy Jesus continued, "Never forget that God sends you people, signs and little gifts each day to help you on your journey through life. These little gifts along the way show you what you are called to do. God sends us people to give us messages that he wants us to hear. Your vocation in life will become clearer to you, the closer you grow to God and the more you rely on Him."

All three puppies were beaming with the biggest, brightest smiles.

"Puppy Jesus," began Lucy, "Do you mean that some day in the future, when we pray about whether we should become a mom, doctor, teacher or nun, that as we grow in our relationship with God, we will know what to do? The Holy Spirit will guide us?"

"Yes! Exactly!" exclaimed Puppy Jesus. "Since you girls decided to take this journey to Paw Peak, you are already heading in the right direction toward holiness and living a virtuous life!"

"Oh wow!" exclaimed the puppies.

"Our final question is, do you know why we've been changing colors and flying since we started this journey up to Paw Peak? asked Lucy.

"This might be surprising to you girls but, you were all chosen to be the protectors of all puppies of the world."

"Is that why we change into rainbow colors with golden wings when our lockets begin to glow?" asked Bernadette.

Puppy Jesus answered, "Yes, the first step to earning your golden wings and rainbow colors is you have to do a good deed or virtue. Then whenever there is an emergency, you say, 'CATHOLIC PUPPIES!' It's at that point you can protect, guide and be an example to all the puppies of the world!"

"Puppy Jesus, did you help guide our parents in choosing the lockets as our first reconciliation gifts?" asked Lucy.

"Yes, I sure did." replied Puppy Jesus. When your parents prayed about what gifts to buy for you, they listened to the Holy Spirit and He revealed the lockets to them. These lockets are very special gifts, you should never take them off." explained Puppy Jesus.

"Thank you SO much, Puppy Jesus!" shouted Lucy, Bernadette and Therese.

Then, Puppy Jesus, heaven and the angel puppies vanished in a flash of light and sparks.

Lucy picked up a little spark off the ground. It tingled in her paws and she put it in her front pocket for safekeeping.

Lucy turned around and looked to the sky and saw Angel Puppy Rose smiling down at her. She gave her a big puppy wave and then ran to catch up with her friends.

About The Author

Bella Velasquez is a 10 year old lover of dogs. She hopes to someday have her own. In the meantime, she spends her time reading books about dogs. She was encouraged to write this book and future series from her Mom. Bella was searching for fictional story books about dogs that also have a Catholic message and wasn't able to find any. So her mom told her to write her own series to inspire young readers like herself!

Bella has three brothers and one sister here on earth and twin siblings in heaven. Her little animal buddy these days is her loyal bunny Coco. She hopes to be an author someday and a veterinarian. Bella's favorite character of this book is Lucy because they have similar personalities and they both have the same locket necklace. Bella hopes to inspire other readers to never give up, to seek God, and live a life of virtue.

In her spare time, when she isn't reading books, she enjoys being an Altar Server at her church. She can also be found goofing around with her siblings, playing sports and spending time with friends.